SERENA
AND
LALOOLEE
FLY AWAY

Also by Rosemary Clunie

Serena and the Little Blue Dog

SERENA
AND
LALOOLEE
FLY AWAY

ROSEMARY
CLUNIE

ZEPHYR

This is a Zephyr book, first published in the UK in 2024 by Head of Zeus Ltd,
part of Bloomsbury Publishing Plc

9 7 5 3 1 2 4 6 8

A catalogue record for this book is available from the British Library.

ISBN (HB): 9781035903788
ISBN (E): 9781035903795

Designed by Jessie Price

Printed and Bound in China by C&C Offset Printing Co. Ltd

Head of Zeus Ltd
First Floor East
5–8 Hardwick Street
London EC1R 4RG
WWW.HEADOFZEUS.COM

To Sir Ben Okri,

whose fabulous flights have inspired me to fly,

with love and gratitude.

'The sky is home to
the dreamers of the earth.'

Leonardo da Vinci

There was once a little girl called Serena who lived in a house in the woods. She loved to walk among the trees, listening to the birds chirping up above. Her special friend was a puppy with a blue paw called Pastel. They played happily together every day.

Even so, Serena dreamed of having an adventure.

Serena and Pastel wandered through the forest looking for one.

As she watched the birds flying high in the sky, she wished with all her heart she could join them.

Suddenly she had a big idea and laughed.

'I'm going to make some wings,' she said.

Pastel wagged his tail as if he understood.

'Then I will fly like a bird.'

Serena collected leaves and twigs from
the forest floor. She made a frame with
the twigs, then wove leaves through
the gaps with long grasses. She
couldn't wait to try her new wings.
Serena climbed onto the branch of
an old oak tree. The ground seemed
far away. Taking a deep breath, she
launched into the air, flapping the
wings as fast as she could. But she
dropped into a pile of leaves, scraping
her knee on a stone. Pastel licked her
hands to make her feel better.

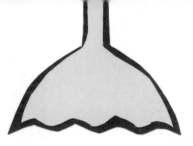

Serena didn't give up. The next
day she thought of another design.
She would use fabric to make the
wings lighter. In her house, she
searched through the cupboards,
gathering scraps of colourful cloth.
Laying them carefully on the floor,
she sewed them to a wire frame.

She strapped on her new pretty wings and climbed onto a tree stump. Taking a deep breath, she jumped and flapped. This time a carpet of thick moss broke her fall. It seemed these wings were not strong enough.

Serena walked round the forest, wondering what to do. She wanted so much to fly! She was about to give up when she remembered the blue stone a wise woman had given her. Yes, that would surely help!

Serena ran home to look for it. She had
put it somewhere safe, as it was precious.
But she had forgotten where! She sat for
a while in her rocking chair, thinking. Her
puppy jumped on her lap and she stroked
him as they rocked back and forth.

Then she remembered!

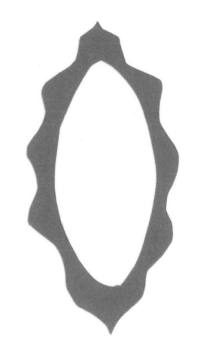

Serena pulled out her wooden chest from under the bed and there the stone lay, its blue light shining, among her other treasures. Holding it tight, she closed her eyes. She waited... and waited and waited... nothing happened.

TREASURE

That night, Serena had a dream. In it the wise woman told her how to make a beautiful pair of wings and taught her a charm to make them fly.

TREASURE

When she woke up next morning,
Serena ran singing into the forest, while
Pastel leaped in circles around her. She
found white feathers tangled in the
bushes and white feathers hanging from
the trees. Big ones and small ones lay
like snow everywhere.

Serena gathered them and sewed them together, as the wise woman had shown her. Then she fastened the shining white wings to her shoulders, climbed the tree stump and sang the magic charm.

To her delight, the wings rose behind her and flapped with great strength.

She was flying!

Serena soared through the air,
higher than the treetops. Soon she
was looking down on her house.
She could see the forest spread
below and the blue river running
through it. Now she could see the
world like a bird!

The air was fresh and Serena felt free as she flew in the bright sky. It felt better than dancing, better than singing! She saw yellow fields and green fields with black roads turning between them. On the horizon were the mountains and the blue castle where the wise woman lived.

She flew on and on.

After a while, she began
to feel tired. She wished her
puppy was with her. The sky
seemed so big and she was
so small.

She wanted to go home,
but she didn't know how.
Suddenly, she felt afraid.
What if she kept flying, and
never stopped? Maybe she
would fly for the rest of her life!
Serena saw a huge tree ahead
and quickly she caught hold of
its topmost branches.

She climbed down to sit on a branch below.

Leaves rustled as the tree swayed in the breeze.

'Hello, Serena!' said a sweet voice.

Surprised, she looked around.

'Hello, I'm waiting for you!' said the voice again.

Serena couldn't see anyone. Then she noticed a
narrow hole in the trunk. She rolled her wings, put
them in her pocket, and squeezed through
the hole. It was dark inside but she saw
light ahead.

She climbed out and stood on a branch looking around.

'Up here, Serena!' said the sweet voice.

She looked up and saw a little girl floating there. She was smiling. Serena instantly liked her, though it was strange to see her hanging in the air without wings.

'Hello,' Serena said.

'Welcome, Serena,' said the little girl.

'How do you know my name?'

The little girl laughed and it sounded like a waterfall.

'The wise woman told me to expect you,' she said.

'Oh! Do you know her?'

'Of course. Doesn't everyone?'

'What is your name?' asked Serena.

'Laloolee.'

'That's pretty. It's like a song,' said Serena.

'It is a song,' explained Laloolee.
'Everything is a song.'

'Oh!' said Serena.

It was all so unusual, even the
colours of the sky and the clouds seemed
different. She wondered if she'd stepped
into another world.

'Why don't you play with me?' said Laloolee.

'What? In the sky?'

'Yes, of course!'

'Shall I put on my wings?'

Laloolee laughed again.

'Everything floats here,' she said. Laloolee drifted down and stood beside Serena on a branch.

'Just let go and the air will carry you. It's perfectly safe.'

Laloolee took Serena's hand. 'I will look after you.'

Serena took a deep breath and let go.

She rose in the air, up, up, up.
It felt like magic.

She saw trees floating past, and
small houses bobbing along like boats
on the sea. Everything was astonishing.

Laloolee let go of Serena's hand and
gently pushed her towards a big woolly
cloud. Serena swam through its soft,
tickly folds, and laughed. This
was fun!

Then they chased each other,
waving their arms and legs to go
faster, as though they were swimming.
They did slow somersaults, curling
round and round and round.

They were playing in a cluster of drifting trees with leaves of many colours, when Serena suddenly stopped.

'What's wrong?' asked Laloolee.

'Listen,' said Serena. 'What's that music?'

'Oh!' said Lalolee, laughing. 'It's the trees singing. They sound like that when they get together.'

Serena clapped her hands.

'It's beautiful!'

They played hide-and-seek in the
clouds, flying among a flock of furry
animals like green teddy bears, tickling
their tummies as they passed. They were
enjoying themselves so much that Serena
didn't notice time passing.

A proud creature glided up to them. It had a swan's neck and head, with branches and leaves instead of wings.

'Oh! Who is that?' Serena asked her friend.

'It's a tree-bird!' said Laloolee. 'Let's go and talk to her.'

The tree-bird turned her elegant neck.

'Hello,' she said.

Her voice was wavy, as if she were under water. Serena smiled.

'Hello,' said the girls together.

'It's good to see you enjoying yourselves,' said the tree-bird.

'It's getting late now,' she went on. 'Shouldn't you be going home to supper and bed?'

'Oh no!' protested Serena. 'We are having too much fun!'

'The sun is going to sleep, so it is bedtime for little ones,' the tree-bird said.

They looked around. The big blue sun would soon be near the horizon.

'I don't want to go home!' said Serena. 'I like it here.'

'You must have someone at home who will miss you?' the tree-bird said gently.

'Yes, my puppy,' said Serena.

Serena pictured Pastel, alone and without food. She felt sad because she hadn't thought of him all this time.

'Yes, you are right,' she said. 'He loves me and I love him, he is my special friend. I can't leave him. I have to go back.'

'Come and play another time,' said Laloolee, taking her hand.

The two girls hugged.

'Oh, I almost forgot!' said Laloolee. 'The wise
woman said to give you a message.'
'What is it?'
'It's about your wings. She said it would help you.'
She leaned over and whispered in Serena's ear.
'Thank you!' said Serena. 'Now I will be able to
fly home.'
They promised to meet again, and
Serena climbed through the trunk
into her own world.

Fixing her wings onto her shoulders, she
repeated the magic words. The wings lifted
her and she flew back the way she had come, past
the yellow fields and the green fields on each side of
the black road. She saw the distant mountains and
the blue castle where the wise woman lived. The
red sun was setting as she flew over her forest
with its curving river. She couldn't wait
to see her puppy.

As she got closer, she heard him barking and saw him running in circles, and she waved. The wings lowered her until her feet touched the grass. The little dog jumped into her arms and she hugged him joyfully.

That night, tucked up in a
warm bed, she held the blue stone
and thanked the wise woman for
her help, for showing her how
to build the wings, and how to
use them. She couldn't wait to visit
Laloolee again in her magical world.

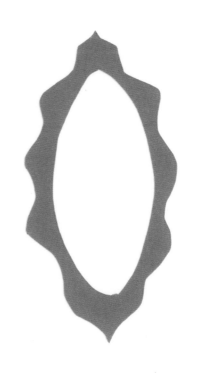

She smiled to herself as she thought of her exciting adventure, and her new friend. Her wings had carried her into a different world, but now she was happy to be safely home with Pastel asleep beside her.

As she drifted off to sleep, her last thought was 'It is not enough to know how to start something, I must also know how to finish it.'

ABOUT THE ARTIST

Rosemary Clunie was born in Scotland, and as a child lived and travelled in the Middle East, Africa and Europe. Books, particularly fairy stories and ancient fables, sparked her imagination. She began painting early, inspired by the beautiful picture books of her childhood, as well as the great masters of art. She became a teller of stories in art and words.

She has always loved animals. Haiku, the little blue dog from Serena's first adventure, appeared one day in the solitude of lockdown and his magical presence prompted Rosemary to write and illustrate her first books for children.

Zephyr is an imprint of Head of Zeus. At Zephyr we are proud to publish books you can read and re-read time and time again because they tell a brilliant story and because they entertain you.

 @_ZephyrBooks

_zephyrbooks

HeadofZeusBooks

readzephyr.com
www.headofzeus.com

ZEPHYR